IF I COULD DRIVE A
GRADER!

by Michael Teitelbaum
Illustrated by Isidre Mones and Mark Mones

SCHOLASTIC INC.
New York   Toronto   London   Auckland   Sydney
Mexico City   New Delhi   Hong Kong   Buenos Aires

ISBN 0-439-36588-0

TONKA is a trademark of Hasbro.
Used with permission.
© 2002 Hasbro.
All rights reserved. Published by Scholastic Inc.
SCHOLASTIC and associated logos are trademarks and/or registered trademarks of Scholastic Inc.

Library of Congress Cataloging-in-Publication Data available

10 9 8 7 6 5 4 3   03 04 05 06

Cover Design by Keirsten Geise
Interior Design by Bethany Dixon

Printed in the U.S.A.
First Scholastic printing, September 2002

My name is Steven. I love to play with my trucks in the sandbox! My favorite truck is a grader.

I pretend that I'm helping to build a new road with my grader. I smooth out the sand so the road is level.

My grader has a cab and big wheels. The cab is where I sit so I can operate the grader. The big wheels help me drive over bumpy surfaces.

The grader's blade sits between the front and back wheels. It can be raised or lowered and turned to the left or right.

When a new road needs to be made, a truck called a bulldozer shows up first. The bulldozer moves lots of dirt and big rocks. Then it outlines where the new road will go.

Once the road is outlined, it's time for my grader to go to work.

Using its blade, my grader shapes and smooths the road surface.

I control the forward movement of the grader with controls in the cab. I also control the movement of the blade.

I raise and lower the blade depending on how high the dirt is. I want to make the road surface smooth and even.

I also want to make sure that the road is not perfectly flat. Instead, it should slope down from the center to the left and the right. That way, rain runs off the road into drainage ditches.

The road is now ready to be paved!

My grader also helps to make the drainage ditches on the sides of the road. These ditches carry the water safely away after a heavy rain. First a truck called a backhoe digs the drainage ditch.

The cut made by the backhoe is very rough. That's where my grader comes in. I use the blade to smooth out the rough cut. Soon the ditch is done.

That's what I would do
if I could drive a grader!